Dear Parent:

Congratulations! Your child is taking the first steps on an exciting journey. The destination? Independent reading!

STEP INTO READING® will help your child get there. The program offers books at five levels that accompany children from their first attempts at reading to reading success. Each step includes fun stories, fiction and nonfiction, and colorful art. There are also Step into Reading Sticker Books, Step into Reading Math Readers, and Step into Reading Phonics Readers—a complete literacy program with something to interest every child.

Learning to Read, Step by Step!

Ready to Read   Preschool–Kindergarten
• big type and easy words • rhyme and rhythm • picture clues
For children who know the alphabet and are eager to begin reading.

Reading with Help   Preschool–Grade 1
• basic vocabulary • short sentences • simple stories
For children who recognize familiar words and sound out new words with help.

Reading on Your Own   Grades 1–3
• engaging characters • easy-to-follow plots • popular topics
For children who are ready to read on their own.

Reading Paragraphs   Grades 2–3
• challenging vocabulary • short paragraphs • exciting stories
For newly independent readers who read simple sentences with confidence.

Ready for Chapters   Grades 2–4
• chapters • longer paragraphs • full-color art
For children who want to take the plunge into chapter books but still like colorful pictures.

STEP INTO READING® is designed to give every child a successful reading experience. The grade levels are only guides. Children can progress through the steps at their own speed, developing confidence in their reading, no matter what their grade.

Remember, a lifetime love of reading starts with a single step!

For Jim, with love
—L.H.
To: Tiffany, Scampi,
Cheyenne, Angie, Chili,
Maggie, Calvin & Chuck
—J.M.

Random House 🏠 New York

Text copyright © 1998 by Lori Haskins. Illustrations copyright © 1998 by Joe Mathieu.
All rights reserved under International and Pan-American Copyright Conventions. Published in the
United States by Random House Children's Books, a division of Random House, Inc., New York,
and simultaneously in Canada by Random House of Canada Limited, Toronto.
www.stepintoreading.com
Educators and librarians, for a variety of teaching tools, visit us at www.randomhouse.com/teachers
Library of Congress Cataloging-in-Publication Data
Haskins, Lori. Too many dogs / by Lori Haskins ; illustrated by Joe Mathieu.
p.   cm. — (Step into reading. A step 1 book.)
SUMMARY: A man's barbecue is interrupted when he is visited by a bevy of dogs from the neighborhood.
ISBN 0-679-86443-1 (trade) — ISBN 0-679-96443-6 (lib. bdg.)
[1. Dogs—Fiction. 2. Stories in rhyme.]   I. Mathieu, Joseph, ill. II. Title. III. Series: Step into reading. Step 1 book.
PZ8.3.H2595 To 2003   [E]—dc21   2002013658
Printed in the United States of America   21 20 19 18 17 16 15 14 13 12
STEP INTO READING, RANDOM HOUSE, and the Random House colophon are registered trademarks of Random House, Inc

TOO MANY DOGS

by Lori Haskins

illustrated by Joe Mathieu

Big dog.

Bigger dog.

Biggest dog of all.

Small dog.

Smaller dog.

Smallest of the small.

Waggy dog.

Shaggy dog.

Doggies in a bunch.

Floppy dog.

Sloppy dog.

Doggies eating lunch!

Sprinkly dog.

Wrinkly dog.

Scratchy dog.

Patchy dog.

Tricky dog.

Picky dog.

Happy, lappy, licky dog!

Spotty dog.

Dotty dog.

Doggies all about.

Howly dog.

Growly dog.

Doggies, please get OUT!

WOOF!